The Ant and the Honey

Published By Parrot Productions Publishing Company, Ltd.
©1994, 1996 Positive Children Programming® Children Educational Television
Programming "Tootee Paradise®"©1992 Parrot Productions LTD® All rights
reserved. Printed in the USA. No part of this book may be reproduced or copied
in any form without written permission from the publisher. All characters and
trademarks are the property of Parrot Productions Publishing Company LTD.

Registration Numbers VA 769-649 2/12/96 TXU 649-106 9/22/94
United States Copyright Office. The Library of Congress.
ISBN 1-890571-26-1

To our children -
our hope for the future

Tootee's Magical Stories
The Ant and the Honey

Adapted from a Persian Folktale

by
Kambiz Azordegan

Illustrated by
Johnny Sajem

The Ant and the Honey

Teaches:

the importance of gratitude.

To The Parents

Welcome to Tootee's Magical Paradise! Who is Tootee? Well, she's the most beautiful bird a child can imagine - and what could be more beautiful than that which comes from the mind of a child?

Tootee wants to help children grow up with beautiful, positive principles, so she flies from Land to Land collecting stories from all over the world to tell the children... stories that come from different cultures. Tootee always tells stories that bring to children positive principles for successful living, designed to encourage them to get along with one another, and to appreciate, respect and accept the differences that make each of us unique.

These principles are brought to life through friendly, animal-world characters and in a way that children enjoy, understand and imitate. Andy, the lovable little ant, may get into trouble in The Ant and the Honey, but in the end, he learns his lesson and goes home a winner, as do all the characters in all of Tootee's stories.

The stories in the Tootee books are the same as those told in the Tootee's Paradise children's television programs that are enhanced with music and dance. The stories are also available on audio and video cassette so that children of all ages may enjoy and learn from them.

Live action version of this story
is also available on *video*.

Books & Video
Ordering Information
(800) TooTee P...aradise
(800) 866-8337

My name is

_____

This is my book.
Will you please read it to me?

Once upon a time there was a forest full of animals. All of the animals worked hard every day and enjoyed their lives. They were happy with what they had.

All except Andy the Ant. Andy worked with his friends to build their nests and gather lots of seeds.

But he was *never* as happy as they were.

He didn't think seeds were very tasty.

One day Andy was carrying the seeds he had gathered back home to the nest.   He felt very unhappy.

Even though he knew his work was important to all the other ants, he just didn't want to gather seeds and especially didn't want to *eat* seeds anymore.

Suddenly, he smelled something
new and exciting!

Andy thought, "What's that?
Something sure smells *good!*"

Andy put down his bag of seeds and looked up. In a tree far above him, he saw a gray beehive.

"A beehive!" Andy shouted. "I'll bet that's honey I'm smelling! I *must* have some of that honey. It's making me so hungry!"

Andy ran up to the tree trunk and began to climb. He didn't stop to think about whether the honey would be good for him. He didn't stop to think how high the tree was. All he knew was that the smell of the honey was making his stomach *grrrowl.*

So up he went. . .

And *d-o-o-o-o-own* he came!

No matter how hard he tried, he couldn't climb that tree trunk!

Now Andy was a very stubborn ant, so he sat at the bottom of the tree and tried to think of a way to get to that hive.

Suddenly, he jumped up and shouted, "Someone help me get up to that honey!

You can have one of my seeds!

Someone please help me!"

Just then, an ant named Wally happened by. Wally was much older tha
Andy and was a different kind of ant. Wally had *wings!*

Wally flew down to Andy. "Hello, Andy! What's the matter?"

"Wally!" said Andy with excitement, "You have *wings!* Will you fly m
up to that beehive so I can get some honey? I'll give you one of my seeds

"What makes you think you need that honey so badly?" said Wally.

"It just smells *so* good!" said Andy, "and I am tired of seeds.
I want something different!"

Wally was worried. "I don't think that's such a good idea, Andy. We're supposed to eat seeds. I know that seeds are better for us."

"Well, what do *you* know?" said Andy. "Anything that smells that good has to be good for you!"

Wally said, "I'm sorry Andy, but I can't take you up there. I wish you would listen to me. Besides, it could be dangerous for you up there."

"I think I know what's best for me," said Andy. "Fly on home if you're not going to help me."

So Wally flew away, sad that
Andy wouldn't listen to him.

He didn't want Andy to be unhappy,
but he didn't want to help
him get into trouble either.

Now Andy wanted the honey more than e

How would he get to it? He thought and
thought but couldn't come up with a way.

Finally, Andy jumped up again and cried as loudly as he could, "SOMEBODY PLEASE HELP ME! I'VE GOT TO HAVE SOME HONEY!"

This time Andy's cries were heard by a fly named Freddy. Freddy liked the ants and tried to help them whenever he could.

"Hi there," said Freddy.
"What can I do for you?"

Andy saw Freddy's strong wings.
"I want to get some honey from that beehive.
Will you take me up there?" he asked.

"Sure! I'll be glad to help," said Freddy.
Freddy was a friendly fly and tried to help
everyone he met. He didn't know the beehive
might be dangerous.

Andy reached for his seed bag.
"Thanks so much Freddy!
Here, have one of my seeds!"

"Oh, no, thank you, I'm glad to do you a
favor," smiled Freddy.

So Andy held on tight to Freddy's legs, and up they went!

As he saw how high they were flying, Andy began to get a little scared. But then the strong, sweet smell of honey made Andy forget about being afraid.

Freddy carefully lowered Andy down on the tree limb.
"Here you are," he said, "just let me know
if I can help you again!"

"Thanks, Freddy!" Andy shouted,
as Freddy flew away to go
about his business.

The entrance to the hive was very dark,
nd Andy couldn't see anything inside,
ut he could hear the buzz-zzzzzzz...
f the bees.

It was a scary sound, but
ndy wanted that honey
soooooo bad
. . in he went!

"It's so dark in here," thought Andy,
as he blinked his eyes and tried to see.
"I sure hope those bees don't catch me!"

Andy crept through the dark tunnels of the hive. He followed his nose toward the honey. The tunnel turned this way and that. The smell of the honey got *stronger* and *stronger*.

Then, suddenly, *PLOP!* . . . Andy stepped into a sticky puddle.

"HONEY! IT'S HONEY! I'VE FOUND IT!"
Andy shouted.

"Oh, this is so good! And there's
so much of it. I could stay here forever!"
laughed Andy, as he began to eat.
Andy *ate* and *ate*. Even when he began
to feel very full, he *ate* and *ate*. But
soon, he began to feel a little *sick*.

Now Andy was scared! "I've got
to get out of here!" he thought.

Andy turned to leave, but he
couldn't lift his legs. He *pulled!*
He *tugged!* He *tugged!* He *pulled!*

It was no use. . . .

Andy was *STUCK IN THE HONEY*

Andy said, "I can't move my legs, this stuff is too sticky!"

All of a sudden the honey didn't seem so good. It was *heavy* and *sticky* and sweet and the smell was making him *dizzy*.

"Help me! Somebody help me! Please get me out of here!" Andy cried. "I'll give you *ALL* my seeds!"

At that moment, Wally happened to be flying back from an errand. He heard Andy's cry for help coming from the hive. "Oh, no, Andy's in *trouble*! How did he get up there? I've got to *help* him."

Wally left his seed bag on the limb and scrambled into the hive.

He found Andy, stuck in the middle of a puddle of honey.

He was *tugging* and *pulling* and *tugging*.

"Andy! What are you doing here?!" said Wally. "I **told** you not to come in here!"

"I know, Wally, I **know**!" cried Andy. "You were **right,** and I was **WRONG,** but please, just get me out of here!"

"Hold on to my legs," said Wally.

Wally flapped his wings and pulled, but Andy didn't budge. Wally was afraid he might get stuck too, but he took a deep breath and flapped his wings as fast as he could and . . .

. . . and . . . and . . . Andy was free!

Honey dripped from his legs, but he was **FREE!**

"Oh, boy, you sure have gained a lot of weight," Wally said.

Wally flew Andy out of the dark hive and into the sunshir The warm sun and fresh air fe good to Andy.

As Wally lowered him down to the ground beside his seed bag, Andy said, "You know, Wally, I don't care if I *ever* taste honey again, but a seed sure would taste good right now!"

Wally laughed. "I hope you've **learned** your lesson. If honey were good for ants, we'd eat it all the time. You should learn to be happy with what's good for you."

"You are right, Wally," said Andy. "That honey wasn't as good as it smelled."

"Let's go home," said Wally.

"Sounds good to me!" said Andy.

So Andy and Wally went back to the nest together. After that day, And
became very good at finding seeds and helping to build the ant nest . . .
almost as good as his friend Wally.

Andy learned a valuable lesson. . . . *We should always work hard to
make our lives better and listen to those who have more experience.*

Questions

1. Was it a good idea for Andy to try to get the honey? Why?
2. Why should Andy have listened to Wally's advice?
3. Why is it good to work together?
4. When you want something, why should you think about whether it is good for you or not?
5. If Freddy was Andy's friend, why didn't he want to help Andy?

Applications

1. Should you listen to a friend who wants to help you do something that is dangerous?
2. When is it good to be stubborn about something? Why?
3. Should you take something that doesn't belong to you without asking? Why?
4. Is a person who wants to stop you from doing something dangerous, your friend?

What have you learned?

_____

_____

_____

_____

_____

_____

_____

_____

Which character do you like best? Why?

_____

_____

_____

_____

Live action version of this story
is also available on *video*.

Books & Video
Ordering Information
(800) TooTee P...aradise
(800) 866-8337